Mandelbrot the Magnificent

D0061844

MANDELBROT
THE MAGNIFICENT

LIZ ZIEMSKA

A TOM DOHERTY ASSOCIATES BOOK

NEW YORK

MANDELBROT THE MAGNIFICENT

Copyright © 2017 by Liz Ziemska

Art on page 120 courtesy of Wolfgang Beyer

Cover by Will Staehle

Edited by Ann VanderMeer

A Tor.com Book
Published by Tom Doherty Associates
175 Fifth Avenue
New York, NY 10010

www.tor.com

Tor® is a registered trademark of
Macmillan Publishing Group, LLC.

ISBN 978-0-7653-9804-8 (ebook)
ISBN 978-0-7653-9805-5 (trade paperback)

First Edition: November 2017

To Benoît,
Thank you for showing me the story
so blatantly hiding between your lines.

Acknowledgments

I am grateful to my editor, Ann VanderMeer, for embracing this unsung mathematical superhero, and to my agent, Renee Zuckerbrot, for guiding him to such a perfect home. Special thanks to the people who helped me shape this book, including Dinah Lenney, Robert Kerbeck, Shubha Venugopal, Lisa Alexander, and Jeff Stockwell. And to Ethan, for his mathematical expertise and textbook loans.

Mandelbrot the Magnificent

ALIETTE IS COOKING CAULIFLOWER once again. My wife favors an old recipe from Brittany. First she blanches it in rapidly boiling water with salt, butter, and clove. Then she fries it in mouton fat with parsley, chervil, and thyme. The curves and angles of her face as she works under the unforgiving light of the kitchen are still beautiful, even after five decades of marriage. I have always been a great lover of geometry. A dash of vinegar and white pepper completes the dish, so much more palatable than the way Mother used to prepare that hateful vegetable. My job was to chop the head into bite-sized pieces (pallid brain leached clean of thought), but it was cauliflower that saved my family that summer in 1944, so over the years I have taught myself to be fond of it.

Aliette sets the plate down next to my laptop, a gift from our children for my eightieth birthday, so I can finally finish my memoirs (or begin them).

"Eat," she says, "while it's still hot."

I take a forkful and admire the curlicues of steam coming off the tiny florets, each part so like the whole, only smaller (an infinite downward repetition). Cauliflower:

my madeleine, memento mori, Mandelbulb, the model
for the fractal theory of nature that bears my name. I take
a bite and the past returns to me with pitiless clarity.

Warsaw

I WAS BORN ON November 20, 1924, at Ulica Mura-
nowska 14, a street that would soon become part of the
Warsaw Ghetto. My brother, Léon, was born fifteen
months later. We lived in a nice fourth-floor apartment
filled with dark wood paneling, richly upholstered furniture, and our most precious possessions, books. The
front entrance and sitting room were dedicated to
Mother's dental practice. All day long patients would
come to our home, everyone from the poorest peddler to
the wealthiest diamond merchant. "Teeth, a more effec-
tive leveler of society than Bolshevism," Mother liked to
say.

I have many happy memories of my brilliant Uncle
Szolem coming over for dinner with his wife. Father
would be working late at his wholesale ladies' hosiery
business, Mother and Aunt Gladys would be busy in the
kitchen, and Uncle Szolem would entertain us with stories about the many mathematicians he idolized: Euclid
and his geometry, Fibonacci and his integers, Poincaré
and his unsolvable theorems, Gaston Julia and his ratio-

nal functions; but it was the story of Kepler's ellipses that truly captured my imagination.

"Johannes Kepler discovered a brand-new law of nature," Uncle Szolem held forth from our best armchair, his manicured fingers pulling shapes out of the air like some metaphysical magician. "Kepler borrowed the conical slice from Apollonius of Perga, and produced a curved shape with not one, but *two* foci.

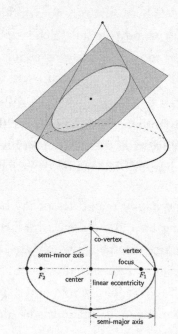

"Then Kepler applied that shape to Aristotle's classical theory of planetary motion, whereby all heavenly bodies, including the sun, orbit the earth in perfectly circular paths . . .

" . . . and instantly all those 'anomalies' that had previously bedeviled astronomers—Mercury retrograde, Saturn return—disappeared, just by replacing a circle with an *ellipse*.

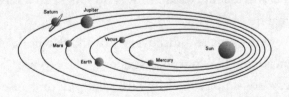

"So simple!" Uncle Szolem snapped his fingers.

Suddenly I found myself astride one of those painted carousel horses at the Warsaw Zoo, the ones that Mother had never allowed me to ride for fear that I might fall off and break my head. Round and round we rode to the plinking sounds of the calliope, until my horse broke free from its circular orbit and began galloping along a tangent line, gaining speed as we shot off into the distance, the wind tossing my hair, tossing the horse's no-longer-wooden mane into my face, and just as we reached the outer perimeter of the park, we were snapped back by the invisible force of that second focal point. Relentlessly, our path curved inward, centrifugal forces tugging at my belly button, as we were pulled back in the direction of the carousel.

I came to rest once again in our living room. The chandelier above my head tinkled in harmony to the molecules that had been displaced upon my reemergence into this world. Uncle Szolem hadn't noticed anything; in fact he was still talking, though I was no longer so interested in what he was saying.

"I want to make a discovery just like Kepler's," I announced, my life's purpose suddenly clear to me, "a discovery so simple, so obvious, that no one else has thought of it."

Uncle Szolem squinted down at me. "Have you been

sitting here the entire time?"

I hesitated. "Yes?"

Uncle Szolem shook his head. "What you wish for is nothing but a childish dream," he said dismissively.

I looked at Léon, who was busy running a toy truck through the interweaving vines of the Persian carpet. *He* was a child, I was not.

"Why can't I be like Kepler?" I insisted. No doubt Kepler had also once ridden the carousel horse to the land of curves.

"Mathematics needs men who are willing to dedicate their lives to her without thought of reward," said Uncle Szolem, selfless mathematician. He stood up and smoothed the creases from his trousers. "Yearning for fame is childish," he said as he left the room.

At six years of age, I had disappointed my uncle, and he had lost interest in me. But I had learned something about myself that day: opposition made me only more determined. (Also, shapes can have very curious properties.)

The Depression hit Poland especially hard and awakened ethnic strife. I was only eight years old, but I already knew that the Jewish situation in Warsaw was desperate.

Uncle Szolem left Poland for Paris, where he had been offered a teaching position at one of the universities. I was sorry to see him go, even though I was still tender about his dismissal of my Keplerian dreams.

Father joined his brother to see if he could build a better life for us in France. Unfortunately, there were no prestigious academic positions waiting for him. Father had been sixteen years old when Szolem was born. Their mother died soon thereafter, so Father had been forced to leave school to take care of his little brother, doing anything he could to make money. Eventually he settled into the rag trade. He never complained about the work he had to do to support his family, though the Mandelbrots, originally from Vilnius, were descended from a long line of Talmudic scholars. Who knows what Father would have become had he been able to continue his studies?

Not long after Father left Warsaw, Hitler became chancellor of Germany, President Hindenburg died, and the political landscape began to deteriorate. Soon there was talk of another war. Mother had grown up in St. Petersburg and survived the Russian Revolution. She knew what was coming, knew the price of hesitating. In 1936, three full years before Hitler invaded Poland, Mother, Léon, and I left Warsaw, taking nothing with us but some essential clothing, family photographs, and the dental equipment that could be easily packed and carried.

(Friends who had been reluctant to leave their park-view apartments, their Meissen china, their illusory dreams of status, did not survive.)

Paris

FATHER HAD RENTED TWO narrow rooms in the 19th Arrondissement, set end to end, like a railroad compartment. There was no hot running water, no bath. The first time Mother entered the apartment, she sobbed inconsolably. By the second day she had recovered and taken control of the household. From then on we were all forbidden to speak Polish. Mother brushed up on her schoolgirl French. Soon she was able to write flawlessly and speak with almost no accent. Father lugged home an obsolete multivolume *Larousse Encyclopedia* and I read it cover to cover. (My accent, however, remained atrocious, like French filtered through Cockney.) I was kept back two grades at school, but my good visual memory served me well and I was soon able to master the French spelling and grammar.

In the fall of 1939, Uncle Szolem received a tenured professorship in Clermont-Ferrand, in the Auvergne region of France, and departed Paris with his family for a small town called Tulle. Father and Szolem seemed to be in agreement about this move, but I was surprised—did my uncle not want to live with us in the same city?

The following spring, my parents took Léon and me out of school and sent us to stay with Uncle Szolem, telling us that there was a meningitis epidemic running through Paris and that the fresh country air would do us good. His new house in Tulle was a simple wooden box built on scrubland near the train station, but it seemed like a palace to slum dwellers like us. Aunt Gladys pampered us and taught us French table manners. My brother and I shared a room, which wasn't ideal, but there was modern indoor plumbing, and out the kitchen door was a small garden. Léon revealed his natural babysitting skills, and he and our new cousin, Jacques, played for hours, which freed me up to pursue my own agenda. I kept hidden my Keplerian dreams and wooed my uncle patiently, incrementally convincing him that I was worth his time. It worked. He became interested in me again and spent many hours talking to me about mathematics and the natural world.

Uncle Szolem began with simple exercises culled from the lycée curriculum: "If Étienne puts a rectangular fence around his cabbage patch, and the patch has a length that's nine meters less than three times its width, what is the perimeter of Étienne's fence if the area of his cabbage patch is five thousand six hundred and seventy meters?"

I found this pedagogical exercise almost insulting in its

simplicity, as my uncle must have intuited because soon we moved on to more interesting thought experiments adapted from one of Zeno's paradoxes:

"Étienne tries to walk to the end of his sitting room, but before he can get there, he must walk half the distance, then a quarter, then an eighth, then a sixteenth, and so on. Will he be able to leave this room and join his wife in the kitchen, where the chicken needs plucking for dinner?"

I didn't have to think about it too long, for the answer seemed obvious to me. "Étienne may never get to the end of his original sitting room, but as he comes incrementally closer to the middle, he kicks up the carpet of our world and creates a space between it and the floor, and as that space grows larger, he will create a parallel farmhouse in which he can live and never have to worry about plucking his wife's chickens again."

Uncle Szolem eyed me uneasily and said, "It's time for you to grow up, Benoît."

———

One morning, a few weeks into our stay, a telegram arrived from my parents. I remember the breakfast Aunt Gladys had served that morning: toasted buckwheat groats with fresh milk and raisins, the aroma so distinct, so warm and nutty. But the look on Uncle Szolem's face set a frozen stone in the middle of my stomach.

"Germany has invaded France," Szolem announced. Aunt Gladys pulled little Jacques out of his high chair and cradled him in her lap.

"Your parents sent this from the train station," Szolem said to me and Léon, a hopeful smile on his normally somber face. "They will arrive in Tulle by nightfall."

What followed was a week of terror and anguish, during which time my brother and I became convinced that we were orphans. I let Léon climb under the covers with me at night, though he kicked like a mule and sometimes wet his bed. Finally, toward nightfall of the eighth day, my parents arrived. There had been no trains; all roads heading south had been clogged with cars and trucks piled high with household goods. My parents had left everything behind in the Paris apartment, except for Mother's precious dental equipment, and walked over four hundred kilometers to get to Tulle, crossing unplowed fields, avoiding main roads, sleeping in abandoned farmhouses.

My parents looked tired and bedraggled when they finally arrived, much older than I remembered them. Mother's lips trembled as she crushed me to her breast. There were crescents of dirt under her fingernails. The stench of her unwashed body brought tears to my eyes, and Father looked like a golem that had risen out of a dried-up riverbank. At that moment there was a tiny shameful part of me that wished I could go on living with Uncle Szolem and Aunt Gladys.

Tulle

TULLE, THE CITY OF SEVEN HILLS, stretches three kilo-meters over a deep, winding hollow created by the con-fluence of the Corrèze River and two of its tributaries. Many streets go straight uphill, with long staircases in stone or concrete. One benefit of this to me was that the girls in Tulle had much better legs than their sisters in Paris. I was fifteen then and quite interested in such things, though unable to act on my interests, due to Mother's strict instructions that we remain inconspicu-ous. She had recovered, my stalwart mother, as she had done in Paris. Her word was once again law.

France was cut into two regions after the invasion. Germany occupied the north, and Marshal Pétain con-trolled the "free" south with his (puppet) Vichy govern-ment. Tulle was technically in the "Free Zone," though not free enough for foreign-born Jews like us, who were not protected by the new laws the way the French-born Jews were. For now. Nevertheless, Uncle Szolem had led us here just in time. It might have been a coincidence, or that he had friends in high places who watched over him, but to my young mind, Uncle Szolem had antici-pated the fall of Warsaw, the fall of Paris, had crossed Europe just one step ahead of the Nazis. His omniscience was unassailable.

Uncle Szolem even found an apartment on the top floor of a small tenement in a little elbow of a village on the very edge of town. As refugees (with his help we registered as Parisians, hiding our Jewishness entirely), we were eligible for welfare and received some furniture and a Franklin stove to cook our food and heat our home. The walls were made of plaster and straw. In winter there were icicles hanging from the window frames. The luxuries of Uncle Szolem's house beckoned. Why hadn't he found us anything nicer? Father had insisted that this was the best we could afford.

The Tullistes, who had a reputation for being un-friendly to strangers, especially Parisians, were kind to us. It was a poor region back then, nicknamed Tulle-la-Paillarde, "the Poor One Who Sleeps on Straw." We no longer had the sorts of possessions that would attract attention or envy, and thanks to Mother's language efforts, we did not seem like strangers (except for my terrible accent, which kept me silent most of the time, though I was bursting with the desire to connect with others). It was from her that I first learned the subtle art of camouflage.

My brother and I went to a school reached by one

of Tulle's endless staircases. It had once been the town house of a local landowner who had been killed in the previous war. The stately rooms of the nineteenth-century mansion had been stripped of their furnishings and crammed full of clumsy wooden desks, but the walls still held their decorative moldings. Sitting in those rooms, I felt like a young nobleman absorbing knowledge amid ancestral splendor.

We had the best teachers from an old lycée in Alsace that had been closed after Hitler incorporated the region into the Reich. Math was taught by a slim, exceedingly pale man named Monsieur Leguay. In another time, he would have been supervising Ph.D. candidates at a university, but there was a war going on, so he was obliged to share his genius with us. He led us through a quick review of algebra, geometry, and trigonometry before scaling the heights of calculus.

Thanks to Uncle Szolem's tutoring, it all came easily to me. I was the best in class on some days, on others the crown belonged to a student named Emile Vallat, son of the town librarian. He was a small, dark-haired boy with an unnatural ability to grind through complicated equations at great speeds. How I envied his agility, his grace. How good it would be to have a friend to bring home and show off to my uncle. And that's when I realized how lonely I had been all this time.

Every morning while I ate my breakfast porridge, I devised in my head various ways to approach Emile, who was always surrounded in school by a circle of worshipful friends. But on my fifth day of school, when I had finally gathered the courage to approach my soon-to-be best friend, Emile Vallat watched me cross the room and said to his allies, loud enough for me to hear, "This one claims to be from Paris, but that face could only come from the ass-end of Europe."

I swerved away before Emile could say anything else, made it back to my desk on trembling legs, the laughter of those jeering boys like shrapnel penetrating the coarse blue wool of my school uniform. Eyes stinging with tears of humiliation, I bent my head and began to draw ellipses into a blank page in my exercise book. (I drew and drew, the lead point of my pencil growing dull and smudgy, until I had created a cool metallic trachea down which I slid and hid for the remainder of the class. Was there really something wrong with my face?)

Friendless, lonely, I looked forward to the weekends, when my family and I would go to Uncle Szolem's house or he would come to us. Food was becoming scarce, but between his extra rations from the university and Mother's ingenuity, an excellent meal was always pulled together. After dinner, Uncle Szolem would quiz me on everything I had learned in class from Monsieur Leguay.

I answered as best as I could, savoring his attention.

One weekend, not long after we arrived in Tulle, Uncle Szolem brought his family to our house, and before I could drag him off to share my latest perfect score, he took my parents into the kitchen and closed the door. When they came out several minutes later, Father looked stricken.

"Your uncle is leaving for America," Mother announced, her expression unreadable (which was odd, because her mobile face never hid how she felt).

"We're going to America?" Of course I assumed we would follow him, as we had done before.

"Not us." Mother shook her head.

"But why?" Who would talk to me about mathematics, my favorite subject, if Szolem left? Not Father, not Léon, certainly not anyone at school. Mother cared only about practical calculations, like the number of molars in an adult mouth or the exact volume of buttermilk necessary to make one pound of farmer cheese.

"Tell the boy," Father said to Szolem, an edge to his voice I had never before heard.

"It's just a matter of time before they push me out of the university," said Szolem. "The war isn't ending as quickly as we thought. Things are about to change for us."

"Us," I repeated, but no one bothered to explain. They didn't have to. We Jews were in the way again, just as we had been in Warsaw. No matter how hard we tried to fit in, we took up too much space, attracted too much attention.

"We will see each other soon," said Aunt Gladys through a smile that did not hide her true emotions: she felt guilty. Cousin Jacques clutched his mother's skirt, his eyes round, couldn't understand why the grown-ups, normally so cheerful when they were together, were now so unhappy with one another.

"Why can't we go with you?" I insisted.

"I have been offered a teaching position in the Department of Mathematics at the Rice Institute, in Texas," Uncle Szolem said calmly. "They are sponsoring my visa."

I looked at Father: *Say something.*

"I have a son," Szolem added, looking away. "I have to think of his safety."

"What about *my* sons?" Father snapped back before Mother could shush him.

Sorting out my feelings, I stood there comparing Father and Uncle Szolem, two brothers so alike, with their high foreheads and small, regular features, except that Szolem was free from Father's stigma of perpetual worry. A freedom that came from his superior education and had been made possible, I reminded myself, by Father's sacrifice.

A circle is a curve with one focus. An ellipse is a curve

with two foci. Torn between the twin foci of Father and Szolem, I wobbled.

Dinner that night was spoiled. Hovering over the table was the growing sense that we might never see one another again. Yet around Uncle Szolem there was a flickering flame-colored aura, as if he were pretending to be depressed about his imminent departure, but in truth he was bubbling over with excitement. (Had anyone else seen it? Was I alone?)

As they prepared to leave, Uncle Szolem took me aside for a little pep talk. "Poincaré said that in most fields a person can be trained to become an expert, but mathematicians must be born," he said, beaming conviction. "Never let anything, or anyone, get in the way of your genius."

It was unsettling to be in his presence now, though I should have been pleased. How far had I traveled in Szolem's eyes, to arrive all the way to "genius" from "childish"? Had I really changed that much, or was it Szolem who had changed? At this close range, I could see for the first time something missing from his shiny, unlined face, something that Father had but my uncle did not: dignity. It was obvious to me now that Szolem was leaving France not for his son, but for *himself,* because an American university had wanted him enough to rescue him from Nazi-occupied France. He was more than just flattered. It was exactly this consciousness of his impending fame that set his eyes ablaze.

"I won't forget." I turned away so as not to let him see the pain I felt at the fall of my idol.

The Book of Monsters

IN LOSING UNCLE SZOLEM, egotistical as I now knew him to be, I had also lost my mathematical sparring partner, so I decided to brave a visit to the public library to see if there were any books that would help me build my knowledge on my own. This was the first time I had ventured out alone, as my accent was still terrible. (Mother had informed the headmaster on the first day of school that I had a debilitating speech impediment, but she couldn't announce that to the whole village.) As the library's original building had been turned into a barracks for the small contingent of German soldiers stationed in our town to "keep the peace," all the books had been moved to the top floor of an apartment building. When I got there I found Madame Vallat, the librarian, sitting behind an old farm table with Monsieur Ricard, the owner of the best hotel in town. They were deep in conversation and hardly noticed me when I came in. I went directly to the stacks and quickly found, to my delight, two entire shelves of books on various mathematical matters. I should not have been surprised given that Emile Vallat, the human calculator, my classroom nemesis, was the librarian's son. I chose three books and brought them to the front desk. As I stood there patiently waiting to be checked out, the librarian and the hotelier continued their argument.

"The Allies only want our interests in Syria and North Africa," said Madame Vallat. She was fair and plump, despite the food rationing. A widow of the last war, somewhere in her early forties, she looked nothing like her son. "Better to stick with Germany."

"If you think Hitler wants France for anything but her resources, you are delusional, Violette," said Monsieur Ricard. He was a fine-boned man in his early sixties, wiry and dark.

"Things will be better when we are allowed to do what Germany has done," said Madame Vallat. "If we don't cleanse the country of all foreigners, Freemasons, and Jews, we French will disappear from France like the Gauls. All that will be left from our culture is the word *merde*."

Heart pounding, I placed the books on the table. Madame Vallat looked me over, visually measuring the width of my temples, the length and slope of my nose. My skin began to itch, as if there were a spider crawling over it.

"How may I help you?" she asked in deliberately archaic French. I was afraid to open my mouth and give her a blast of my Cockney French. Would she denounce me, the way her son had done in class?

"Leave the boy alone." Monsieur Ricard pushed my stack of books closer to Madame Vallat.

Never taking her eyes off me, she stamped all three and pushed them back.

"Shoo," said Monsieur Ricard.

"Merci," I mumbled, tucking the books under my arm and forcing myself to walk *slowly* down the stairs. Out on the sidewalk I felt nauseated from the knots in my stomach. Was this how Uncle Szolem had felt every day at the university? Did he also encounter people who did not like how he looked? I felt pity for him now, and shame at the cold and formal way I had treated him when we said good-bye.

———

Later that night after dinner, I sat down and started looking over my books, so perilously acquired. There was one volume on advanced calculus, another on infinite sets, and a third entitled *The Book of Monsters*. I opened it and on the flyleaf encountered a quote from Uncle Szolem's favorite mathematician:

> These functions are an outrage against common sense,
> an arrogant distraction. But logic can sometimes make
> monsters, and it is the beginner that would have to be
> set grappling with this teratologic museum.
>
> **Henri Poincaré, 1899**

Teratology, I knew that word from Mother: it was the study of congenital abnormalities, like the two-headed calf. *Terato,* Greek for "monster" or "marvel." I flipped through the book and encountered not monsters, but many beautiful shapes. Like the snail coil of the Archimedean spiral:

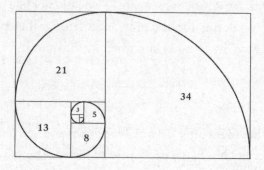

The crystalline elegance of the Platonic solids:

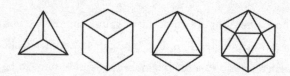

But then things got really strange with Cantor dust,

which looked like the tallit prayer shawl worn by Father on Yom Kippur, with its twined and knotted tzitzit, a reminder of our obligations as Jews to heed G-d's commandments:

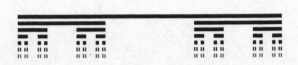

And the Koch snowflake, which looked exactly like a snowflake in its middle stages, but in its early and late stages began sprouting triangles, which sprouted more triangles, and more triangles, until the triangles became movable arms that could manipulate space and time:

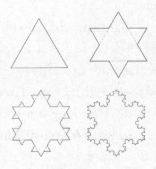

Then there was the Sierpiński triangle, which looked like a geometric Cronos that had eaten up its tiny offspring and now had a stomachache from all those pointy apexes sticking into its intestines:

I stayed up all night thinking about those infinitely nesting triangles (like those Russian dolls Mother used to have in her dental office to amuse her younger patients while she drilled their teeth). I vowed to master *The Book of Monsters,* no matter how long it took me. It would be my atonement to Szolem for accusing him, in my heart, of selfishness and vanity.

The following morning I went off to school feeling light-headed from my sleepless night, but not tired.

Everything I saw—the trees, the buildings, the hills surrounding the town—had an extra shimmer of possibility around it. How wonderful the world was, how full of mystery! Maybe today I would stop cowering in the back of the classroom. Maybe if I said something brilliant, Emile Vallat and his friends would overlook the shape of my face. Perhaps we could even start doing homework together.

The school day went by slowly, medieval history, Latin, and zoology of no interest to me whatsoever anymore. Finally Monsieur Leguay came into the room. He lectured for a bit on how to find the volume under a curve, all very basic, reasonable stuff. I didn't even bother to take notes, but when he finally put down his chalk and asked if there were any questions, I quickly raised my hand.

"Could you please explain the Sierpiński triangle?" I was showing off, I won't deny it.

Monsieur Leguay looked surprised and thought for a bit. "No," he finally said. "That subject is beyond the scope of this class."

I was disappointed but knew better than to insist. In those days, students did not challenge their teachers as they do now.

"Any further questions?" Monsieur Leguay looked around the room.

Emile Vallat, who had been staring at me the entire time with his little amber fox eyes, now raised his hand. "Could you please explain, Monsieur Leguay, why it is that Jews in the Free Zone are not required to wear yellow stars on their clothes?"

The entire room went silent, so silent that I was certain they could hear my heart beating through the thick wool of my jumper. I kept my eyes on Monsieur Leguay, wondering what he would do. Would he defend me? Would he order Emile out of the room? Monsieur Leguay kept staring down at his desk. His face grew pink, then red, and then completely white. The bell rang. All the boys grabbed their books and ran out the door into the courtyard, where the ordinary world, as I could see through the classroom window, had not lost its radiance.

I remained at my desk, hoping for a word from Monsieur Leguay, any word at all, but he just packed up his bag and walked out of the room. I was crushed. Another door had slammed. What had I hoped for? An apology? More praise? A replacement for Uncle Szolem? I could almost hear his voice in my head: *That is a childish dream.*

The Hausdorff Dimension

AFTER THE INCIDENT WITH the yellow stars, I vowed never to speak in class again, though I continued to turn in my homework, as I had always done. If Monsieur Leguay was one of the *poisson pourri*, as Mother called the French collaborators, then I did not want to attract any more attention in his class. I stayed home after school with *The Book of Monsters*, which I had copied out by hand, like those Talmudic scholars in Vilnius, before returning it to the library. Deeply absorbed with my pathological shapes, I paid very little attention to the pathological events of the "real" world.

When Germany invaded the Soviet Union in the summer of 1941, Mother became almost cheerful. "Russia kicked Napoleon in the *tuches*," she said, abandoning her proper French for one choice Yiddish word, "now let's see what she will do to Hitler."

"Things will be easier for us once German troops are pulled out of France and sent east," Father agreed.

We had heard about the Jewish doctor living in a nearby village, the one who had been denounced by a jealous rival and deported to a concentration camp. For this reason, Mother had been hesitant to resume her practice. Emboldened by the news of the Soviet invasion, she took out her dental equipment for the first time since we came to France, crossed the landing, and knocked on the door of the only other apartment on our floor. Monsieur Hubert, a retired engineer, lived there all alone. He had been complaining of toothache to his downstairs neighbor, Madame Popova, a retired dance instructor. We could hear everything through those flimsy walls, every marital squabble, every sneeze (and many other things, too). Mother pulled Monsieur Hubert's tooth free of charge, then she went downstairs and pulled one from the odoriferous mouth of Madame Popova's ancient Pomeranian.

Word spread of her skills, and soon Mother was on a first-name basis with Vincent, the butcher, who had terrible gums. He set aside special cuts of meat for us. Chickens were out of our reach, but a rooster could be made palatable if cooked long enough with tarragon, peppercorns, and onion.

Madame Derrasse, who owned the bakery, received a new bicuspid made of gold melted down (by Father, with a desktop smelting forge fashioned by Monsieur Hubert) from her wedding band (her husband had passed away during the middle years of the Third Republic). From her we received every Friday a loaf of braided brioche studded with brandy-soaked raisins.

As my parents grew more comfortable going out into the village, I was drawn inward, to my little corner of the living room and the book of mathematical shapes that I had copied out by hand. One night, after several weeks of fruitless puzzling, I began to sense that I was on the verge of a breakthrough.

After gulping down the oxtail stew Mother had set in front of me, I began to etch the Archimedean spiral in the thin brown gravy with the tines of my fork, counting out the Fibonacci sequence as I drew the overlapping curves: $1+1=2$, $2+1=3$, $3+2=5$, $5+3=8$, $8+5=13$, $13+8=21$. I could feel the brittle surface of the plate becoming spongy, the fork piercing through the flat plane of the tabletop, my fingers sinking down into an undiscovered realm of pure . . . until Mother took my plate away.

"You're too old to play with your food!" she said as she dropped it into a pail of sudsy water.

The spell was broken, and yet the feeling lingered, that indescribably delicious sensation of penetrating a new realm. That chipped blue plate had been given to us by Aunt Gladys before she left for Texas. It had ordinary, real-world dimensions. How was it possible that I could stick practically my entire hand inside it (perhaps even my whole body)?

The kitchen was hot and stuffy. The backs of my legs stuck to the chair. I left the table and hurried back to the corner of the living room, pulled out *The Book of Monsters*, and flipped through the pages until I found what I was looking for: the *Hausdorff dimension*. It's what all the monstrous shapes, including my dinner plate, had in common.

Hausdorff's innovation was a simple one. Previously, the concept of dimension had been thought of as something that *extrudes* into space and could be described by a set of coordinates, x, y, z. A point (x) has the dimension of one; a line (x,y) has the dimension of two; and a cone, cube, or sphere (x,y,z) has the dimension of three. This is the ordinary kind of dimension, the Holy Trinity of Euclidean geometry. It is called *topological dimension,* or D_T.

But when Felix Hausdorff encountered the geometric

monsters, he quickly realized that D$_T$ would never work for them. For instance, if the Peano curve (another shape monster) is like a pot of soup to which you can keep adding handfuls of noodles, what happens to the hundredth handful? The hundred thousandth handful? All those noodles can't go into the third dimension because the Peano curve is two-dimensional, and the noodles can't go into infinity because the curve is bound at the top, sides, and bottom by the square (or whatever other shape) that it inhabits. It defies logic and all known laws of the universe. And yet the noodles must go somewhere....

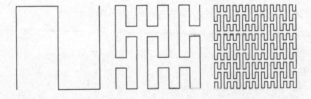

Frustrated by the limits of mathematics, Felix Hausdorff decided to create a new kind of dimension, one that went *in* instead of *out*. He wasn't the first person to think about dimensions in this way. The Oxford mathematician Charles Dodgson, better known as Lewis Carroll, had the same ideas. Only after Alice drinks the

potion and becomes small is she able to open the door
and enter the garden.

The Hausdorff dimension, D, is that garden.

D is where I would one day hide my family.

Life Under the German Occupation

WHEN THE ALLIES GAINED a foothold just across the Mediterranean in North Africa, Germany abandoned the pretense of the Free Zone and moved south to occupy all of France.

To commemorate the day, Emile Vallat (at least I assumed it was him) left a pig's snout on my chair. Did it hurt me? Oh, yes, it did, because I had still hoped we would become friends one day. We both loved math—wasn't that enough to cancel out our differences? Apparently not. The pig snout made me feel queasy, but I tried not to show any sign of weakness, so I forced myself to stand there and contemplate the offering. Then I actually began to admire the tender symmetry of the fleshy circle with its delicately flared breathing holes. With a handful of dried peas and a yellow onion it would make a fine soup. But not for us.

I am impervious to your taunts, I wanted to say to Emile. *You have your handful of cronies, but my friends are numbers and they are legion.* I tore a page from my notebook, wrapped up the snout, and tucked it into my satchel.

Later that day, I fed it to Madame Popova's Pomeranian. The dog chewed the snout ecstatically with its remaining teeth, while the mistress (blond, berouged, seventy) fed me stale caramels and complimented me on the width of my shoulders.

A *Kommandatura* of veterans from the last war and wounded soldiers shipped back from Russia moved into Monsieur Ricard's Hotel St. Michel, along with a small Gestapo division. As a gesture of goodwill, their senior officer, a dentist from Bonne, began offering free dental care. We heard about this from Madame Derrasse, who came to our house to deliver some plain country bread (no more braided brioche, too risky) and to assure us that no one but Dr. Mandelbrot would be allowed to touch the mouths of the inhabitants of our little corner of Tulle.

But Mrs. Vallat was clearly delighted by this news, because soon Emile showed up at school with the first set of dental braces ever seen in the Corrèze region. With his vulpine face and silver-clad teeth, he looked positively carnivorous. He liked to flash that metallic grin at me during class, a warning to keep silent.

I have often wondered why Emile waited so long to denounce me. Perhaps it gave him great pleasure to keep me close, yet muzzled (a trained bear on a delicate leash), so that he could savor the torture he was certain I felt, knowing the solutions to all those math problems in class but not being able to say them.

After the Gestapo arrived, my parents no longer left the apartment. Patients started coming to us, quietly, despite the increased risk. Quotas were going up; the local police were looking closer into people's backgrounds, searching for hidden Jewish ancestors. Families were taken away every day; sympathizers didn't fare much better. Nevertheless, they came: a farmer's wife, Vincent the butcher, an apprentice who worked for Madame Derrasse at the bakery, a maid at the Hotel St. Michel, they all slipped in after dusk and sat under the kitchen light, heads tilted back, mouths open, as Mother stood above them wielding her glinting instruments. In payment they would leave whatever food and supplies they could spare. I was reminded of Warsaw during the Depression, except for the fact that at any moment one of these villagers could decide to report us to the authorities. It was a risk, but Mother insisted that it was worth it.

The food we received we shared with the dwindling occupants of our apartment building (many had died or moved away to a more desirable part of town). During the day, Father and Monsieur Hubert would clean, sharpen, and sterilize the instruments. From donated silver teaspoons and various bits of jewelry they would fashion crowns and bridges so that our friends would also have glittering mouths.

While my parents were busy building a wall of neighborly support around us, I was too preoccupied with preparations for our year-end examinations to pay much attention to the Germans in our midst. For those students who managed to pass the notoriously difficult exams, there would be two additional years of school that would then qualify them to apply to the university. I had to pass those exams. Uncle Szolem, wherever he was, would expect nothing less from me. Why else had Mother and Father sacrificed everything to bring me here, a place of relative safety? All winter long, while Mother practiced her clandestine dentistry and Father devoted himself to the custom tailoring business he ran from the kitchen table, I studied Latin, philosophy, physics, geography, and history. *The Book of Monsters* would have to wait until after the exams.

One night when I was up late studying, Mother came to me with a slice of mandelbrot, still warm from the oven. I hadn't seen one of these cookies since Warsaw.

"You will do well on your exams"—Mother set the plate down next to my books—"but not *too* well. Do you understand?"

Where had she gotten the butter, the almonds? Madame Derrasse must have needed some fillings. "I understand," I said.

Not only Emile Vallat but also my mother wanted me to hide my talents. Maybe it would be better if I stopped studying altogether. Maybe I should go out and fight instead.

There were rumors going around about hooligans hiding in the countryside. They were delinquents, gangsters, escaped convicts, Communists sent over from Spain, but also French citizens who were tired of living under German occupation. They were supplied by the Allies in a series of nighttime parachute drops over the French countryside. Well armed, the hooligans were coming out at night to blow up bridges, burn down factories, demolish train tracks, ambush supply convoys—anything they could do to sabotage the German war machine. Silently we cheered for them, these *maquisards* (named after the *maquis,* or "brushland," in which they lived), but we also trembled. There were posters all over town threatening severe reprisals for collaboration with the "terrorists."

Several boys from my class had gone missing, though Monsieur Leguay never acknowledged their absence, simply skipped over their names during roll call. Which of them had run away to join the freedom fighters (or "rebels," as the Vichy government and the Germans called them) and which had been denounced?

How wonderful it would be to *do* something rather than pretend to be invisible. Maybe I should join them instead of memorizing Latin verbs.

For weeks I stayed in the house like a dutiful son, went straight home after school, even though I was growing restless from the boredom and isolation. Books and homework assignments were my only companions, besides Léon, who was fifteen months younger and therefore didn't count. There was no one my age I could talk to, no one who shared my interests (mathematics was Léon's worst subject). Finally, one Sunday in early spring, when my family was still sleeping and the rest of Tulle was in church, I packed a rucksack with my handwritten copy of *The Book of Monsters,* a wedge of bread, and some cheese and slipped away.

The note I had left on the kitchen table said that I had gone out to forage for mushrooms, which was my original plan. As soon as I hiked up into the hills above Tulle, I was overcome by the beauty of the sky, which was as clean and blue as the Virgin Mary's mantle (I say this in honor of France's fabled Catholicism, as this is a French story, set in a French meadow, during a beautiful spring day in France). Birdsong sifted through the fragrant air as crickets harmonized in the underbrush. Wildflowers speckled the lush damp meadow: honeysuckle heavy with bees, rhododendron, ragged mallow, periwinkle, primrose, peony, and above it all, the mauve blur of almond blossoms.

Everywhere that I saw flowers, Uncle Szolem would have seen numbers. Archimedes ruled the architecture of the pinecone, the unfurling of the fern frond, the distribution of florets in the head of a sunflower, he would have said. I could write the formula from memory:

$$\theta = \frac{2\pi}{\phi^2}\, n, \quad r = c\sqrt{n}$$

Φ being the symbol for the golden ratio, the sacred number that links the Archimedean spiral with Fibonacci's integers, 0, 1, 1, 2, 3, 5, 8, 13, 21, 34, 55, 89, 144 . . .

"God is a mathematician," Uncle Szolem had said to me on our long country rambles (which seemed so long ago). I had shown him that I could do the numbers, that I could be his equal, given time and some additional tutoring—so why hadn't he taken me with him? As soon as these traitorous thoughts invaded my mind, I could picture Father bending into the light, threading the needle, straining to make perfect stitches. Shame on me. Ungrateful, is what I was, and *selfish*.

And furthermore, G-d is not a mathematician! Look at the clouds—they are not spheres. Mountains are not cones, light does not travel in a straight line, and bark is not smooth. Nature is rough and beautiful, not rigid and symmetrical, like the world of numbers in which Uncle Szolem lived.

As I ran my hand over the trunk of a chestnut tree, I disturbed a moth I had not noticed. It settled onto a nearby branch, folded back its wings, and became invisible once again. Holding my breath so as not to disturb the creature, I leaned closer to examine the ragged distribution of color on its powdery wings: beige-blush-brown, beige-blush-brown, all over the moth, all over the tree. How clever of the moth to color itself to match the sun-dappled tree bark. What keen pleasure I felt in unmasking Nature, the archdeceiver!

I looked back at the clouds, mountains, and trees: perhaps there *was* an order to this apparent chaos, one that Uncle Szolem and his mathematicians could not even begin to understand. Sitting in the shade of that moth-sheltering tree, I took out my notebook and began filling page after page with equations (not the ones Uncle Szolem had shown me, but the ones in my *Book of Monsters*), searching for a pattern in the weave. Until my eyes grew heavy and I decided to take a nap. A quick one.

When the drone of a large insect finally woke me, it was full dark. The moon was just a crescent sliver in an inky sky seeded with stars, more stars than I had ever seen. It was late. I cursed myself for the worry that I was causing Mother. A shadow fell across the stars, diminishing their brightness, the silhouette of an ice-cream cone descending diagonally toward a nearby hillock. I grabbed my things and started running toward what I thought would be its landing spot.

The parachute came down into a raspberry thicket, its payload a large wooden crate. I was just beginning to untangle the chute from the thorns (what a pretty dress Father could make for Mother from the silk) when a circle of men stepped out of the shadows. I saw the dirt-smeared ovals of their faces, heard the clinking of rounds chambered into guns, pointed at me. But I wasn't scared. Somehow it all seemed as if I were still sleeping beneath that tree, dreaming of mottled wings.

"Who are you?" said a dark-haired man. He was older, possibly forty, with a Spanish accent, possibly a Communist. "What are you doing here?" said a boy holding a gun with shaky hands. I recognized him from school, the son of a shoemaker. A third one, somewhere between a boy and a man (eager to prove he was the latter), cried, "He's a spy!" A fourth, bespectacled, spit into the grass. "He's a Jew!" I knew what he meant: Jews are not supposed to have nationalistic feelings. They weren't fighters, because they had no state to fight for and therefore could not be trusted.

You can trust me, I wanted to say to them, *it doesn't matter where I'm from,* but the men and boys kept inching closer with their guns, and all I could do was to keep staring at the girl who stood behind them, a beautiful dark moth with liquid brown eyes and mahogany curls. I had seen that girl in the village, walking on the arm of a German officer. Tonight on this desolate hillside she was unescorted, unarmed, and even more luminous in her camouflage of brown wool and muddy corduroys than in the printed dresses and genuine silk stockings she had worn on her "dates." She winked at me, and then the one with the glasses took me roughly by the arm and began to lead me away.

"Let him go." Another man stepped into the clearing, and at first I had trouble recognizing him, so out of place was he in this setting. It was Monsieur Leguay, and he looked as etiolated as ever, though no longer frail, now that he had shrugged off his habitual stoop.

He looked at me as if trying to decide my fate, and I became aware of the sheer bulk of my shoulders, my plowman's hands, how much taller I stood than most of the boys holding me at gunpoint. What a good addition I would have made to this band of outsiders, if only I had been the son of a different mother. I shrank myself smaller, ashamed at being able-bodied but unwilling to put myself at risk.

"Go home, Mandelbrot," Leguay finally said, shouldering his rifle. "You have a lot of studying to do if you're going to beat Vallat next week."

And just like that, my life became interesting.

My Keplerian Moment

LATER THAT NIGHT WHEN I got home and explained
to my frantic parents that nothing had happened to me,
that I had merely fallen asleep, and that I would never
go out again, I savored all that I had learned that day:
Monsieur Leguay had failed to defend me against Emile
Vallat *not* because he agreed with that little anti-Semite,
but because he had not wanted to draw attention to himself and blow his cover! And furthermore, by mentioning
the upcoming exams in front of his *maquisards,* Leguay
had instructed them to understand that I was *not* a coward for not joining them, but that I was a scholar, and
that my talents were best utilized elsewhere. One day
when the war ended, this country would need mathematicians. And finally, by mentioning Emile *specifically,*
Leguay showed me not only that he had been tracking
my academic progress (or lack thereof), but that he was
encouraging me to work harder, to surpass Vallat and
take my rightful place at the head of the class. Satisfied
that I had figured everything out, I opened my books and
set joyfully to the task of becoming excellent.

The dreaded exams, when they finally arrived, were like a particularly satisfying military skirmish. I pulverized Latin, destroyed philosophy, annihilated physics, buried geography. Biology was no match for my knowledge of the physical world. History was but a fairy tale I had memorized in childhood. At last there was mathematics, the final exam of the week. I had consumed the textbook, rewritten all my notes, particularly the ones I had scribbled down while rambling the countryside with Uncle Szolem, listening to his treatises on complex polynomials. I was ready.

The morning of the math test I put on a clean white shirt, combed my unruly thatch of hair, and walked slowly to school, savoring the gentle warmth of the late-spring sun. When I entered the classroom, Emile Vallat was already seated at the front, reeking of lavender soap. I went to my customary place at the back and began ranking freshly sharpened pencils into ascending order of length.

Monsieur Leguay strode into the room in a swirl of black robes. Without saying a word, or even glancing at us, he rolled up his sleeves and began cleaning the blackboard. My classmates fidgeted in their seats, scratching at mosquito bites, cracking knuckles. Almond petals floated in through the open window.

Monsieur Leguay turned around and addressed us.

"Today's examination will consist of as many problems as the class can solve in one hour." We groaned in anticipation of some impossible task. "You may use your notebooks to work on them, but the answers must be given orally."

Leguay turned to the board and began filling it with mathematical symbols.

$$\int_0^\pi d\theta \int_0^{2\pi} d\phi \int_0^1 d\rho\, (\rho^2 \sin\theta)$$

I told myself not to be fooled by the pleasing trinity of those integral signs, which recalled to me the supple backs of girls strolling down the street on the arms of German officers, laughing over their shoulders at the tall, galumphing Warsaw Jew clutching an armful of books, his only friends in this village of monsters those same books attained at great peril from the library, which was run by a gorgon, hurrying home (along the opposite side of the street) so that his mother wouldn't worry.

Or perhaps *I* was the monster, the impossible being that should not exist, not in this world in which I would never be allowed to be good enough, never reach the brilliance (because Mother told me not to) of Johannes Kepler, or Uncle Szolem, or even Emile Vallat.

But truthfully, ruminations aside, what Monsieur Leguay had written on the board was the worst equation I had ever seen! Nothing that Uncle Szolem and I had talked about on our rambles through the Tulle countryside had prepared me for this. Nothing that Leguay had taught us in the past year came even close. Was it a trick? I tried to talk it out to myself silently, maybe a verbal recitation would penetrate a hidden corner of my mind, but it sounded even worse than it looked: "an integral over the variables theta (from zero to pi), phi (from zero to two pi), and rho (from zero to one), with an integrand of rho squared times the sine of theta."

I glanced around the room to see how everyone else was doing. None of the other students seemed to know where to begin; they just sat at their desks like dazed chickens. Except Emile Vallat. His head was down, the sinews of his skinny neck strung tight as bowstrings, scribbling steadily in his little blue notebook.

I glanced at Monsieur Leguay, who was seated behind his desk reading a local newspaper, swatting flies. This was the end for me. How would I survive the humiliation of disappointing not only my parents and Uncle Szolem, but also this man who had saved me from the *maquisards*?

Just as I was beginning to ring the death knell of my career in mathematics, something strange happened to those integrals, sines, cosines, pis, alphas, thetas, and phis: they floated away from the blackboard and swam around in the air above my desk, lit by the rays of the sun, like fireflies dancing above a flower-filled meadow. I began to feel dizzy and forced myself to look away, to think of something else or, better yet, nothing, to empty my mind entirely. Quiet surrounded me like a gentle mist. I felt calm in this thought-void, in the stilling of normal perception. Then, on the very edges of consciousness, I began to detect a little flutter. Soon it invaded the edges of the non-space in my empty mind, kicking up density, curving inward, taking shape, until I finally *saw something,* and once I had seen it ($4*pi/3$, of course!), I could never *unsee* it.

My hand flew up.

Monsieur Leguay looked surprised. "What is it, Mandelbrot?"

"Monsieur," I began, unable to keep the grin from my face, "I see an obvious geometric solution to the problem. What you have written on the board is nothing more than an overly complicated way of stating the volume of a sphere!"

My fellow students held their breath. Emile put down his pencil but did not turn around to look at me.

Leguay glanced over his shoulder at the board, then back at me. "Correct."

The room exploded in whispers. Emile closed his notebook.

Monsieur Leguay erased the board and wrote out another, even more elaborate equation. It was no match for me. At this point the numbers were yielding up to me their three-dimensional counterparts as readily as foam bubbling out of a pot of boiling milk.

"The volume of a three-dimensional shape created by a plane bisecting a cone at an angle of thirty degrees," I announced, remembering Apollonius of Perga.

Leguay wrote another equation.

I solved that one, and the one after that, as my classmates stared at me, eyes wide, lips parted, marveling at the magnificent exploits of their once mute Mandelbrot. Surprisingly, they all seemed happy for me. Except Emile Vallat, who looked at me with eyes as cold and lifeless as a pair of amber nuggets stuck into the sand at the bottom of the North Sea.

It's just a trick, I wanted to say to him. *Absurdly easy, anyone can do it.*

But I knew that it wasn't a trick. This was *it,* the event that I had been waiting for: my Keplerian moment had arrived. If only Uncle Szolem had been there to witness it.

———————

"I have something amazing to tell you!" I said as I burst through the door.

"Go wash your hands," said Mother as she leaned over the kitchen table. "We'll be eating soon."

Only when she straightened did I realize that she had been lighting candles. Four, to be precise: one for each of us. Her gray-streaked hair, which she normally wore in a twist at the nape of her neck, was covered by a white lace shawl.

"We're celebrating the Sabbath?" We hadn't done that since we left Warsaw, not wanting to advertise our Jewishness (the Friday arrival of Madame Derrasse's faux challah notwithstanding).

Father got up from his sewing table and came over to measure the circumference of my neck. "Do as your mother says, it will be dusk soon." Then he ran the tape from my right shoulder down to the first knuckle of my thumb.

Mother waved her hands over the candle flames to extract their illuminative power, then cupped her hands over her eyes and prayed, *"Barukh ata Adonai Eloheinu melekh ha-olam."*

"What's the occasion?" I asked. Was all this for me? Had they already heard of my triumph in the classroom?

"You're the occasion," said Léon. I hadn't even noticed

him, but there he stood at the sink, placing wildflowers into a pretty blue vase.

"You told them?" I was upset that he had stolen my fire. And furthermore, how had he known? Léon and I ran in different circles. It would be more accurate to say that he had *friends,* while I had only my *Book of Monsters*.

"The whole school is talking about it," said Léon, "probably the entire town."

"Bring those flowers over here," Mother snapped.

"It's not my fault," Léon whined, though he obeyed without hesitation.

"It's nobody's fault," said Father.

"But you don't even know the best part," I said, still not grasping the situation. "It was as if the numbers were speaking to me directly and—"

"When will they post the class rankings?" Mother cut me off.

"Monday afternoon," I said. "But I already know: I will be the first."

"Maybe not," Mother said to Father. "There's still some chance they might fail him, or at least knock him back a few levels."

"There is no chance," I protested. "I answered every question perfectly!"

"We can't be certain," said Father. "It's not worth the risk."

"Then we will have the weekend to prepare." Mother turned to Léon and me. "And you two will leave first thing Monday."

"Leave?" Had my entire family gone insane?

Mother set her raptor gaze on me. "Remember when I told you to do well, but not *too* well?"

I could feel my face turning red with shame, but wounded pride made me want to push back. "What kind of mother tells her son to do anything less than his best?"

Mother reared back as if I had slapped her. How awful I was at that moment, but I so badly wanted to be praised. She turned away and began preparing a salad of bitter greens.

Léon looked at me with awe (was it really possible to talk to Mother that way?).

"I *like* our school," he said, suddenly bold. "Let him go. I'm not going anywhere."

"I'm not going anywhere," I said.

"You *should* go," Léon said to me. "Without you, they'll leave us alone." (I didn't blame him. It couldn't have been easy being my brother.)

Father got up and stood between us. "Why ruin the little time we have together?"

I went over to Mother and placed a protective hand on her shoulder. I had grown that year, she seemed tiny in comparison. "I'm sorry I spoke to you that way," I said softly, "and I know that you're upset because you're worried, but you have nothing to fear, Monsieur Leguay will protect us."

Mother turned around. "Who is this Leguay?"

"That day I told you that I went out to gather mushrooms, and you got mad at me because I came home after dark? Well, that's because I came upon Monsieur Leguay in the *maquis*," I said, "and it turns out that he's not just my math teacher, but an officer in the Resistance."

"I knew it!" Mother pulled the shawl off her head and threw it on the ground.

"Leguay is the one who told me that I should try to beat Emile Vallat," I said, happy that she finally understood me. "He encouraged me to be the best in class. My success is helping the war effort. It's an act of resistance, a way of showing the Germans that we are not afraid." I was improvising now. It felt good.

"He set you up," Mother said.

"Listen, Trotsky, not everything is a conspiracy." Father patted Mother's hand affectionately, though I could tell that he too was concerned.

"I saw the men and women he commanded," I insisted, though at this point I was mostly trying to convince myself (such was the power of Mother's skepticism). "They had guns, they will protect us."

"Resistance fighters don't care about people like us," Mother said dismissively. "They only care about glory. It's romantic for them to play soldiers under the stars. I met many of those types in Russia during the revolution. They all had boring lives before the war, as teachers, clerks, mechanics. Guns make men feel heroic, and equal."

"Maybe he couldn't help it," Father offered. "Having such a brilliant boy in his class, it's irresistible. Maybe for once he just wanted to reward his best student, even if he was a Jew."

I noted with pleasure and surprise that Father took my side, though the whole situation was painfully confusing. Had I really been a pawn in Leguay's game? What was that game? To punish Vallat? Did it have something to do with his mother, or her lover, the owner of the Hotel St. Michel? In any case, my path was now clear.

"Whether or not Leguay betrayed me, I am staying here," I said.

"So am I," said Léon, though he did not look certain. "We'll protect you."

"If that's your decision, then tomorrow you will go see the rabbi in Brive and tell him so in person," Mother said as she brought the salad to the table.

"What rabbi?" At no point during our exile had my parents ever mentioned a rabbi.

"The rabbi who has already bought your tickets to Lyon, paid your tuition at the new lycée, and arranged your new identity papers," said Mother. "The rabbi who helped Szolem escape to America."

I turned to Father, my only possible ally: "I'm not leaving you, not the way Szolem did."

As soon as those words were out of my mouth, I regretted them. *Forgive me.* I tried to catch Father's eye, but he turned away from me.

"We should eat," he said, and folded up the traveling suit he had been making for me.

The benefit of this unfortunate exchange, in which I impugned Father's ability to take care of his own family, was that I suddenly became docile.

"Let's eat," I said, grateful for the distraction.

Mother had performed the miracle of the loaves and fishes, but instead of the traditional challah bread, a pair of Romanesco cauliflowers commemorated the manna that had fallen from Heaven upon the wandering Israelites. Bright green and ornately textured, they looked like the jewel-encrusted baubles crafted by Fabergé for the Romanovs (another doomed family). Lamb neck (Vincent the butcher was getting creative) cooked with wild garlic completed the meal. The smell alone should have drawn the Gestapo to our door, but to me it all tasted like sand.

G-d, Mathematician

BRIVE-LA-GAILLARDE, "BRIVE THE BOLD," is a prosperous market town twenty-nine kilometers southwest of Tulle. The road to Brive being mostly downhill through numerous twists and switchbacks, I was able to make the journey in a little over an hour using Monsieur Hubert's rusty bicycle. It had just stopped raining when I rolled into town. The streets were coated with damp pink cherry blossoms, giving them a gruesome aspect, as if the cobblestones were carpeted with flesh.

I rang the bell at an elegant villa on the avenue Turgot. A stern-faced girl opened the door and led me upstairs to the second floor, where my benefactor sat in his book-lined study. Rabbi David Feuerwerker was thirty-two years old the day I met him, but despite his beard and balding head, he looked more like a young pugilist than a man of G-d. He shook my hand and we sat down on a pair of chairs upholstered in faded green velvet. The girl served us tea in tall, gold-veined glasses. The rabbi offered me sugar, a rare luxury. I accepted one cube, though I wanted three. Already I was beholden to him.

Born in Geneva, Rabbi Feuerwerker spoke French with a Swiss accent. His ancestors had come from a small town in Transylvania. He was an expert in Aramaic, particularly its Syriac dialect, the language spoken by another famous rabbi, Jesus of Nazareth. All this I would learn later. For now I was focused on trying to figure out how to tell him that I could not accept his generosity.

"I have heard great things about your mathematical abilities," he said.

My resistance began to melt under the warm breath of praise. "Who told you?"

"Your father."

How? I wondered. Did they write letters to each other? But more interesting, it was the second time in two days that I discovered, with chagrin, that my father had more depth to him than I had previously realized. I had always assumed he was just a tailor and a merchant, a man lacking the sophistication to comprehend the mathematical world Uncle Szolem and I had shared.

"That's why your parents thought it would be wise to send you to a school that could better develop your natural talents," the rabbi continued.

"That's not why they're sending me," I said, feeling my face turn red with shame. "In any case, I plan to remain in Tulle."

"I will cover all expenses," he countered.

"My parents are old. We are at war. This isn't the time for selfishness," I said, feeling very mature.

"Selfishness is not the issue here." The rabbi's dark eyes probed my resolve. "Neither is shame." He poured me another glass of tea and offered more sugar. I accepted two cubes. "The only shame is in humanity's unquenchable desire to destroy itself."

I popped a cube into my mouth and crushed it between my teeth. The concentrated sweetness made my eyes water.

"Creation and destruction," the rabbi said after a few moments of silence. "Are you familiar with the concept of *tikkun*?"

I could feel the sugar rising through the roof of my mouth, setting my thoughts a-skitter. "No." We never talked about religious matters at home, only practical things like food, survival, and academic achievement.

"Any positive act is *tikkun*," he explained. "Simple kindness, a scientific discovery, the creation of a new masterpiece in the realm of art, music, dance, literature, even going to a different school to continue your mathematical studies: these are all examples of *tikkun*."

Nonsense, I thought, though the exact word that came to mind is unprintable. "Like my Uncle Szolem," I said quickly, "who abandoned us to pursue his mathematical studies in Texas?"

The rabbi nodded. "Szolem was far too talented to remain in France. We had to keep him safe."

Anger made me feel huge in this room of glass-lined bookcases. "And what about my parents, are they of no value?"

"It's not me doing the choosing," he said, "it's the Americans. They know what's happening to us here, and in the rest of Europe, but they don't want the whole rabble of us appearing on their shores. Here and there they make their selections—a musician, a painter, a physicist, a mathematician. Only the best will get on the ark. Become the best, and you can save yourself."

"And my family," I said.

The rabbi lowered his head. The gesture could have been interpreted as a nod. "In the meantime, go to Lyon," he said. "Study hard, learn everything. Your parents will remain hidden in Tulle."

"Hidden where?" Would Madame Popova hide them under her voluminous skirts? Could Madame Derrasse bake them into a pie?

Rabbi Feuerwerker got up and retrieved a sheet of paper from his desk and handed it to me. I glanced at it and found a familiar shape.

"Uncle Szolem had one of these hanging in his study." The diagram consisted of ten nodes labeled with Hebrew letters joined together by twenty-two connected paths.

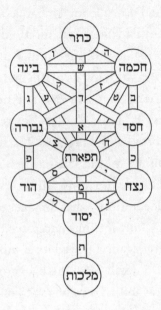

"What can you tell me about it?" asked the rabbi.

"Not much. I asked Uncle Szolem about it, and he said it was just a decoration."

The rabbi raised an eyebrow. "It's called the *sefirot*."

"So what is it?" I asked, annoyed that Szolem's evasion now made me seem foolish.

"*Sefirot* is Hebrew for 'emanations.' According to the Kabbalah, it is the filter through which the *Ein Sof*, the Infinite, reveals Himself into the physical and metaphysical realm. Some people believe that it contains esoteric knowledge passed down from Archangel Raziel to Adam and Eve after they had been cast out of Eden, so that they might use it to regain entrance into Paradise," said the rabbi. "Szolem was studying its mathematical properties."

"Clearly neither Adam, nor Eve, and not even Szolem were able to solve it," I said, "unless Texas is Paradise."

The rabbi snorted with laughter. "I have never been to Texas, so I cannot say." He leaned forward and tapped my knee, which made me jump a little. "When you look closely at this 'decoration,' what do you see?"

I put aside my hurt feelings and forced myself to look down at the *sefirot* again. I traced its complicated treelike structure while somewhere in the background, sounding very far away, the rabbi's voice began to recite in Hebrew: *Kether, Chochmah, Binah . . .*

Curves began to spin out clockwise like the little vortex created by pulling the plug in the chipped claw-footed tub in our communal bathroom. The curves drained out of the page and splashed down onto the polished wooden floor of the rabbi's study until it appeared as though we were sitting at the edge of a deep pool filled with something more viscous than water, yet so completely clear that I could not actually perceive it as a substance, but more like an *absence,* its contours discernible only at the borders of itself and ordinary space.

I kept staring into that invisible yet discernible stuff, could feel it oscillating through the soles of my shoes.

Dimples began to disturb the non-substance like a sudden spring downpour, setting its non-surface boiling (what is the inverse of boiling?) . . .

Chesed, Gewurah . . .

But there were no raindrops here, only words, with their consonants and vowels, diphthongs and fricatives, hitting *ping, ping, ping!* . . .

Tiphereth, Nezach, Hod . . .

. . . causing even greater turbulence, until the viscous non-substance crested its banks and came sloshing up over the cuffs of my trousers, soaking me to the knee with numbing cold (not *cold,* more like numbness, nonbeing). I could feel the polyrhythmic thrumming of the rabbi's words in the bones of my legs, my hips, climbing up my spine, as if all the atoms of my body, my blood, bones, sinew, and even my eyelashes were dissolving into a densely swarming mass of neutrinos, winking on/off, on/off, on/off, like fireflies.

I panicked and used all my will to launch myself out of the primordial soup, like a pike leaping out of a lake to catch a fly, and suddenly I found myself back in my green velvet chair, with the rabbi examining me closely.

I patted myself down, making sure that all parts of me were back in the mundane world of men and jackets and chairs. "Have I been here the entire time?" I asked.

"As much as anyone is anywhere," the rabbi said calmly, but he had a twinkle in his eye.

"Your recitation," I began, testing my voice, "it was very nice."

"The ten *sefirot* have beautiful names"—the rabbi nodded—"but what shapes did you see when you looked inside?"

"Curves," I said. How else could I describe what I had seen? "Or maybe, ripples."

The floor beneath my feet had resumed its solid woodness. There was a damp spot on the toe of my right shoe, but that could have been from the rain-soaked flower petals. My brain hurt and I felt oddly disjointed, like a chicken that had been taken apart for stewing.

"How many curves did you see?" asked the rabbi.

"Hundreds." (What else could I say?)

"Szolem was only able to see fifty." He leaned back in his chair and crossed his arms, clearly delighted.

"Really?" A small twinge of pleasure at besting Szolem brought forth a smile, though I quickly suppressed it.

"I too was once good at math," the rabbi said wistfully. "When I was a boy I could add numbers in my head. Stacks and stacks of numbers, without making even one mistake. But then I contracted scarlet fever, and my abilities disappeared, though I was never able to see the *sefirot* as you or Szolem do, even at my best."

I shrugged and felt my shoulders pop back into their sockets. If what I had just experienced meant being good at math, I wished it on nobody.

"It is a gift," he insisted, noting my doubtful expression.

A curse.

"One that you must protect," he added.

"Thanks for showing it to me." I tried to hand the *sefirot* back to the rabbi.

"You used shapes to solve mathematical equations in class." He pushed it back to me.

I nodded. Was this really such an extraordinary feat? It seemed so obvious to me.

"Can you reverse the process?" he asked.

"How so?" I said.

"Can you extract the mathematical formula for the *sefirot* by examining its curves?"

An equation that describes a set of infinite overlapping curves that contain within their center a matter-dissolving core activated by sound waves? Not even Monsieur Leguay would assign such an evil problem. "Not sure I can. Why would I want to?"

"Every mathematical genius since Pythagoras has tried to solve the *sefirot*," said the rabbi. "Isaac Newton believed that it was the key to the transmutation of matter. Others believe that it's a metaphysical puzzle box constructed to contain the *Ein Sof*, the Most Hidden of the Hidden, more commonly known as G-d. But I shouldn't have asked you. It's too much for a young boy."

"How close did Uncle Szolem get?" I asked. Few mathematicians had ever made an important innovation past the age of twenty-five, I wanted to say. At sixteen, I was in my prime.

The rabbi leaned forward and unclasped his boxer's hands. "Maybe if you go to school and work hard, you can join your Uncle Szolem in Texas and ask him yourself."

"We're back at the beginning," I said, startled by the sudden turn of our conversation away from esoteric matters.

"That's what happens when you go around in a curve." The rabbi stood up.

"So what do we do now?" I said, trying hard to hide my disappointment.

"Remove yourself and your brother, and your parents will not be touched," said the rabbi.

"Will you promise to protect them if I promise to work on the *sefirot*?" I said, unwilling to leave it on faith, though I had already decided to leave Tulle.

The girl came back into the room before he could answer me. She was about twelve, I guessed, with delicate features positioned in the center of a round pugilist's head. She glanced at the diminished sugar bowl.

"Say hello to your father for me," said the rabbi as he delivered me to his daughter.

———

As I rode out of Brive into the jasmine-scented, cricket-mad dusk, I felt the suffocation of the rabbi's study leave me. And though the realization that he had simply been humoring me still stung (he had no right to treat me like a child, distracting me with pretty mathematical toys), that thrumming presence I had "seen" in the floor of his study was real. It was not a hallucination. In fact, I could still feel a residual quiver coming from inside the breast pocket of my jacket, where the *sefirot* was safely tucked, oscillating harmoniously with the beating of my heart.

I didn't need the rabbi's praise of my "mathematical abilities" for them to be real, either. I had my own confirmation. But why *hadn't* Uncle Szolem told me that he had been working on the *sefirot*? Had he wanted to keep it a secret, or had he thought that I wouldn't be able to understand it?

How wonderful it would be if *I* could solve it! How old had Kepler been when he solved the problem of planetary motion? I could certainly try, as I would have even fewer friends in that school in Lyon (fewer than zero?). At least I would have no enemies and therefore no distractions. If nothing else, the *sefirot* and its infinite curves would make a fine new shape for my *Book of Monsters*.

And shapes were everywhere that evening: in the parabolic swoops of insect-chasing swallows, in the roiling buttermilk curdles of the clouds, in the bobbing, windswept heads of chamomile daisies, as dense and golden as a teeming beehive. And as I crested the hill above the town I had gotten used to calling home, I could not help noticing that the topography of Tulle, with its brainlike infoldings and outcroppings, resembled the Romanesco cauliflower Mother had served for dinner.

Garments of Concealment

WHEN I FINALLY ARRIVED home that night, Mother was sorting through our clothes, picking out the most essential items to bring to our new school. Léon was in the living room composing a good-bye letter to some girl he had met in the village (where did he find the time for girls?). Father was at the kitchen table sewing buttons onto matching plaid suits that were supposed to transform us from a pair of Polish immigrants fleeing deportation to young noblemen traveling for pleasure. No one bothered to ask me how it went with the rabbi, which offended me.

I sat down on the couch next to Léon and pulled out my *sefirot*. I began to stare at the ten nodes and twenty-two interlacing pathways, willing them to unspool a puddle of magical magma onto the floor of our humble apartment, hoping to show them all, but the incident that had occurred at the rabbi's house failed to repeat itself.

"What are you doing?" Léon nudged me. "Shouldn't you be helping Mother?"

"Shouldn't you?" I said, turning away from him.

Why hadn't it worked? Had it been the rabbi who had performed the miracle of the curves and splashes? Had he tricked me into thinking I was special and therefore "worth saving"? And then I realized what was missing: *In the beginning was the Word.* Sound was missing, the rabbi's sonorous recitation of the names of the *sefirot,* but on my copy they were written in Hebrew and I could not read them.

I glanced up at Mother, who was now standing in the kitchen pulling together another meal out of last night's leftovers. She spoke French, Polish, Russian, and a little German, but she was a scientist, a secular intellectual, and despite the Sabbath prayer that had rolled so easily off her tongue, I doubted that she could help me. Then I looked at Father, who had just bitten the thread attaching the last horn button to my coat of many colors. Maybe he had picked up some Hebrew during his merchant days in the Warsaw Ghetto.

I went over and showed him the paper. "Rabbi Feuerwerker gave me this diagram, but I can't read it."

"Let me see." Father put down the needle and picked up a pencil. Without hesitation, he drew a fresh *sefirot* on the back of the page and began to fill in the name of each *sefira,* translating from the Hebrew as he wrote each one: "*Kether* (the Divine Crown), *Chochmah* (Wisdom), *Binah* (Understanding), *Chesed* (Mercy)."

I could feel the vibrations through the table as the pencil scrawled over the page. Couldn't he also feel them? I was too afraid to ask, in case I got sent to bed with a hot-water bottle. "How do you know all this?" I asked instead.

"Seven generations of Mandelbrots were Talmudic scholars in Vilnius," Father said as he continued to fill in the nodes with *Gewurah* (Justice), *Tiphereth* (Beauty), *Nezach* (Eternity), "but when the family moved to

Poland, we lost some things. Or let them go."

"Who taught you?" I asked.

"My father," he said as he kept writing and the table kept shivering: *Hod* (Glory), *Jesod* (Foundation).

"Why didn't you teach me?" I asked.

"It didn't seem like useful knowledge for the modern world," Father said as he filled in the bottom-most node, *Malchuth* (G-d's presence in the World). "You should learn how to sew. I can teach you."

Ignoring his kind offer, I kept my focus on the drawing. "So what *is* this thing?" I asked, wondering if he knew more than the rabbi.

Father picked up the pencil again and began drawing curves. "That's a very difficult question to answer." Dozens and dozens of curves spun out of his pencil, overlapping, interlacing, so many curves that I began to worry that the tabletop might dissolve at any moment and we would fall through. "Some people believe that the *sefirot* is an instrument by which the ten aspects of the Divine can be perceived in the physical plane," Father began, "but my father taught me that these"—he tapped at the tangle of curves with the point of his pencil—"are actually Garments of Concealment."

"Concealing what?" I asked.

"The Most Hidden of the Hidden." Father looked at

me as if I were slow.

"G-d?" I said.

Father shrugged. "That's a simple word used by those who would be terrified if they knew the whole story."

I nodded, having experienced a tiny bit of that terror in the rabbi's study. And then I had a vision of a delicate moth concealed by the clever pattern of its own wings, hidden in plain sight against the mottled tree bark by layers and layers of overlapping color, each tiny spot of color so like the whole.

I looked closer at the *sefirot*. Though it was obviously just a diagram of an esoteric symbol, could it be that these ten nodes that had sprouted ten to the tenth to the tenth (ad infinitum) number of curves, like a pond in a rainstorm, were just a shape monster, another version of the Koch snowflake or Sierpiński triangle, a geometric creature that depended on the Hausdorff dimension for its prodigious proportions? Is that what I had seen in the floor of the rabbi's study, the Hausdorff dimension in action? Then what was the *sefirot* itself? A diagram for the structure of the universe? A map that showed the way back to Paradise? A puzzle box containing G-d?

"If this drawing was the blueprint for an engine," I asked, "which of these *sefirot* would be the switch that turned it on—*Kether,* the Divine Crown? *Chochmah,* Wisdom?"

Father pointed to the very center. "*Tiphereth,* Beauty."

"Why beauty?" I asked.

"Because beauty combines compassion with strength," said Father. "It is the *sefira* of transmutation."

"Like the transmutation of a two-dimensional object"—I tapped the drawing—"into a multidimensional Garment of Concealment?"

Father reached up and stroked my face. "You're a good son."

Not as good a son as you deserve, I wanted to say to him, but if I said it, I would cry, and there was too much work to do for that sort of thing. Instead I asked, "May I borrow your tape measure?"

———————

That night, while everyone slept, I went out into the hallway and contemplated the entrance to our apartment from the point of view of someone standing on the landing. I ran my hand over the door, collecting dark green paint flecks on my fingertips. I memorized the patterns of the water-stained plaster of the wall beside it, noting the traces of countless grimy hands, the bits of straw sticking out from the wattle. I could see the pattern in the pseudo-randomness of the stains and chips. Any moth could mimic it.

I went back inside and pulled out my *Book of Monsters*. Flipping through the pages, I found the chapter on *tessellation,* the process by which a shape is repeated over and over again (*iterated*) to create a plane without any gaps or overlap, sort of like laying tile. In order to mimic the dirt patches of the walls in the hallway, I thought it would be best to use Koch snowflakes of two sizes and two degrees of complexity as my "fundamental region."

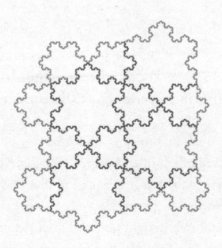

Then I could fill each snowflake, at random intervals,

with five different degrees of the Peano curve.

If I iterated these shapes over the entire surface of the door, it should blend perfectly with the surrounding wall. In theory.

No, there was no time for self-doubt!

I measured our door and plugged the dimensions into my perimeter equation (the equation that told the Koch snowflakes when to quit making more snowflakes). Then I performed three straight hours of calculations, making sure that the tessellations fitted together perfectly, filling them in with variegated Peano curves. Then I rolled up the tape measure, gathered my pencils and papers, stepped back into the apartment, closed the door, and whispered one magical word: *Tiphereth*.

Nothing happened. The heavens did not open up, lightning did not strike, G-d, "the Most Hidden of the Hidden," did not speak to me from His primordial broth. And yet, I was too superstitious to open the door and see whether or not my mathematical spell had actually worked. I forced myself to trust myself, the way Father seemed to trust me now, which was amazing to me, because I could count the number of our significant interactions during my entire childhood on one hand. Father had always been too busy making money to pay attention to me. He had done it for us, so that even within the confines of the Warsaw Ghetto, we had everything we needed. Now it was time for me to do something for him.

They arrived first thing Sunday morning, while the rest of Tulle was still at church. Mother saw them from the kitchen window: four German soldiers climbing the hillside to our building, led by a small dark boy with the narrow face of a fox.

Was it perverse kindness that had inspired Emile Vallat to give us the Sabbath? For he certainly could have brought them to our house on Friday, right after the math test. Or did he take the precaution of first going to church and receiving the sacrament before committing the sin of consigning innocent people to their deaths? Either way, we were trapped. Our apartment building was perched at the very top of a hill, at the very edge of the town. The only way out was the same steep and narrow path that was now blocked by men in black uniforms and swastika-emblazoned armbands.

"I knew this day would come," Mother said bitterly. The look of genuine despair on her face almost made me lose my nerve.

"You did this to us!" Léon looked at me with hatred.

"Hush!" said Father.

"We have to stay calm," I said, trying to believe myself.

"We have to hide!" Léon cried as he started pushing the couch in front of the door.

"Get in here!" Mother grabbed me by the sleeve and tried to stuff me into the broom closet. "We'll tell them we have no children. Maybe they'll just take us and go."

"Maybe we can climb out the window," said Léon as he shook out his bedding and started tying sheets together.

"It's six stories, we'll never make it." Father took the sheets away and refolded them. "Your brother has a plan, don't you?"

I nodded at Father, pushed the couch back into place, and made them sit down.

We heard a door slam below.

Madame Popova's Pomeranian began yapping hysterically.

"They are coming up the stairs!" said Léon as he tried to get up.

"We need to keep very still," said Father as he grabbed Léon's hand and pulled him down.

My family watched me in terror as I got up and walked over to the door—the sound of military boots growing louder than the yapping—and opened it carefully. Monsieur Hubert hated to throw things away, so in addition to his rusty bicycle, I found a pair of old galoshes from the pile of debris by his door, also a shovel, an empty rabbit cage, and various other odd bits to drag in front of our door. Then I closed it, making sure once again *not to look*.

"We're hiding behind our neighbor's trash?" Léon wailed.

"Shhhh!" Father whispered.

Mother's lips were moving in prayer, but there was no sound coming out of her mouth. I sat down between my parents and took their hands. Mother's fingers were trembling, but Father's hand was warm and dry. He believed in me.

The soldiers arrived at the landing just outside our door. We could hear the low murmur of their voices, the clink of their guns as they examined Monsieur Hubert's door, checking the number against the one they had been told contained Jews. They knocked anyway. Thank God Madame Popova had recently convinced our neighbor to start attending mass, for appearance's sake, as Monsieur Hubert was a devout atheist. The Nazis didn't care for Catholics, but they hated Communists almost as much as they hated Jews. We waited for the pounding on our door, but nothing happened. Where was Emile? I could not sense him out there. No doubt he had run home after leading the Nazis to our building. Coward.

The Pomeranian kept yapping. The clock above our kitchen sink ticked loudly. Would our breathing give us away? Would the enchanted tessellations hold? Had I missed anything in my calculations?

The squeak of boots; the clink of metal against metal.

"They're leaving!" Léon whispered.

"No, they're just going down one flight," I whispered back.

Mother cried softly as they came back up and then climbed one flight above ours. The attic door opened with a screech, slammed shut. We could feel more than hear as they tore the place apart, searching for us. Then the soldiers came back, cursing, joking, *"Der kleine Scheiße Kopf,"* and clattered all the way down the stairs to the ground floor, out the door. Only then did Madame Popova's Pomeranian stop yapping.

We sat still for a moment, relearning how to breathe.

"Stupid Germans." Léon laughed with relief, tears in his eyes. "They don't know how to count."

Oh, they do, numbers are their specialty, but I have disappeared our door.

Mother regained her voice. "Get ready to leave tomorrow at dawn."

"Yes, Mother."

The Fractalist

I HAVE OFTEN WONDERED why the soldiers did not simply break down our neighbors' doors and search for us when they could not find our apartment number. My only guess is that they were acting on orders not to antagonize the civilian population, to keep them calm, complacent.

That would all change in a matter of weeks.

After the Gestapo left our building, I had renewed faith in my ability to protect my parents using my mathematical skills. Only now I had to build a different kind of mathematical camouflage, something that would protect them for weeks and months, if not years, and yet allow them to move around a bit in the neighborhood, as Léon and I would no longer be there to do the shopping for them.

After the great starvation of the previous winter, our neighborhood gathered together and started making plans for a longer war. Vincent the butcher acquired a pregnant sow and now there were piglets, six of them, too adorable to contemplate eating, but this was something

I could not think about now. Madame Derrasse kept five chickens under lock and key in a roomy mesh enclosure behind her bakery. They were good egg layers, secure in their avian knowledge that they would never be eaten. Madame Derrasse's niece kept rabbits. Everybody had a vegetable garden these days, from the poorest farmer to the most exalted aristocrat. The basement of our apartment building was stocked with root vegetables, jars of preserved tomatoes, and several hefty blocks of burlap-wrapped cheese made from the milk of a cow my parents would no longer be able to access. Like the Tatars who were our distant ancestors, we had laid by several sacks of dried apples. The stream beside our house ran clear with cool water from which an agile fisherman could pull the occasional silver-mottled trout. In the few hours remaining before our dawn departure, I had to do all that I could to protect our fragile Eden.

Once again I reached for my *Book of Monsters* and reread my favorite part of the Poincaré epigraph:

Logic sometimes makes monsters.

That Emile Vallat hated me so much for being better than him at math that he had denounced me to the Germans was logical, but monstrous. That the German people who suffered so much after losing the previous war would choose a charismatic leader like Hitler who promised to return them to their former international status was logical, but monstrous. That the Jews were blamed for everything that went wrong in the world ... well, that's where logic broke down and became doubly monstrous, or monstrous². In any case, this was not why I had turned to my *Book of Monsters*. What I had been searching for were my notes on Gaston Julia.

Gaston Julia, who was still alive at the time of these events, was a French mathematician whose nose had been blown off during the previous war. Despite the inconvenience of having to wear a mask over his mutilated face, he went on to write, at the tender age of twenty-five, a 199-page essay entitled *Mémoire sur l'itération des fonctions rationelles,* describing the iteration of rational functions. This had been Uncle Szolem's favorite piece of writing. Julia became so famous for his essay that he was awarded the Grand Prix de l'Académie des sciences. But despite his early fame, his work was largely forgotten.

I prayed this would never happen to me.

Right up to the time Uncle Szolem left for Texas, he had been trying to revive and continue Julia's work. As far as I knew he had made little, if any, progress. After my success with the *sefirot*-powered Koch snowflake/Peano curve tessellated two-dimensional camouflage door skin, I believed I could do better than Szolem.

I began by thinking about the definition of an iterated rational function: an equation that uses its solution to plug back into itself, like a dog chasing its own tail (and the ancient symbol of the uroboros that the Zoroastrian magi used to cast their spells). I decided that I could use this sort of equation to build volume into a shape that was similar in its camouflaging abilities to the one I had made with the tessellated snowflakes, but this time I would pop it out not only to 2-D or 3-D, but into D, the Hausdorff dimension, a dimension that was bigger on the inside than the outside, so that I could hide not just our door, not just our apartment, but our entire neighborhood, which was shaped, much like the rest of Tulle, as I had noticed on my ride home from Brive, like *cauliflower*.

Or, more specifically, a single *floret* of cauliflower, which was exactly the same shape as the vegetable itself, a small part so like the whole, a fragment, a (what would you call a partial fraction?), a . . . *fractal*.

Yes, fractal was a good name. Now all I had to do was figure out the formula for the shape of a cauliflower floret and I would soon have a template for the tessellation that I would need to create my Hausdorff dimensional neighborhood-within-a-neighborhood *infolding* in which to hide my parents.

Going back to Gaston Julia, I found that his basic iterated equation was: $Z_{n+1}=Z_n^2+c$, where "c" is a constant.

Well, I would have written that same function more simply as $Z = Z2+c$, and in order to mimic the shape of a cauliflower floret, thereby mimicking the shape of our little corner of Tulle, what better number to use than the universal constant that rules the architecture of the pinecone, the distributions of branches on a tree, the coiling of a seashell, a fern frond, and the spiral arrangement of seeds on the head of a sunflower: the golden ratio,

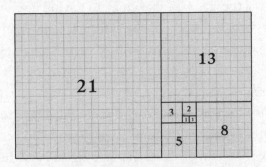

which can be described by the formula following:

$$\Phi = \frac{1+\sqrt{5}}{2} = 1.61803339887...$$

That night, while my family slept (my mind always works best when all the other minds are switched off), I once again borrowed Father's tape measure and began plotting out my Z variables.

The distance from the center of the kitchen table to the front door.

The distance from the front door to the lobby.

The lobby door to the sidewalk. The sidewalk to the bottom of the staircase that clung to the hill upon which our building was perched, like a cairn, teeming with life.

The bottom of the staircase to Vincent's butcher shop, then a little farther, to the bakery owned by Madame Derrasse.

The distance from the front door to the little stream at the bottom of the hill, where my parents could get fresh water in the event of an aerial bombing and a disruption of the municipal water supplies. The distance from the bottom of the staircase to the end of the alley located between two factory buildings that connected our little hidden elbow of a neighborhood to the more desirable parts of Tulle.

I took all these measurements, and several incremental others, and plugged them into $Z=Z^2+c$, and I did it over, and over, and over again, filling pages and pages of laborious calculations, in ever widening "spirals" of Hausdorff dimension, D, reciting the entire *sefirot,* just to be extra sure that it would work: *Kether, Chochmah, Binah, Chesed, Din, Tiphereth, Nezach, Hod, Jesod, Malchuth.*

As our last night in Tulle faded into salmon-pink dawn, I added the finishing touches to a semiporous (to allow for gas exchange) fractal canopy using my *sefirot* dimension generator (the way I would one day use a 3-D printer to create a scale model of the fjords of Norway). Inside their mathematically enclosed neighborhood (an invisible pocket sewn into the space/time continuum), my parents would be able to move freely, while remaining completely invisible to the outside world, because it was bigger on the inside than the outside by a factor of three, as the Hausdorff dimension is more capacious than our own and also more resilient. This should have been enough, given my parents' limited mobility. I would have liked to make it bigger, but the construction of a fractal canopy roomy enough to cover all of Tulle would have required thousands if not millions more calculations, the kinds of calculations Emile Vallat could have cranked through in no time, but Emile was my enemy and the reason why I had to build that fractal canopy in the first place. Thus life iterates onward, one mistake following another, like a dog chasing its own tail. I did leave two holes for the river to run through, so as not to inadvertently flood my creation. Hadn't I thought of everything?

From our top-floor kitchen window, I gazed out onto the courtyard below. The same crows nested in the linden tree across the street, because they were real; but the mist curling into the creases of the foothills across the valley had more in common with a painted scrim than an actual product of nature. That said, I couldn't tell the difference, and hopefully, neither would my parents. I only prayed that it continued to appear beautiful and rough, like nature itself. Would my construction hold until I could come home and dismantle it? I had no idea, but I put my faith in mathematics, because in mathematics there were no Jews, no Muslims, Hindus, Buddhists, Freemasons, or Zoroastrians. There were only numbers, real and imaginary, predictable and reliable, and, above all, dispassionate. Numbers did not separate mankind into artificial problem sets.

The Tulle Massacre

FOR SIX LONG WEEKS, our past and heritage obscured, my brother and I lived at a lycée located in the suburbs of Lyon, which was a beautiful city, a real metropolis, unlike Tulle, with ancient cathedrals and elaborate villas built by Renaissance silk weavers. Recently it had become infested with Nazis, so we hardly saw it. Topographically, Lyon consisted of two large hills guarding a flat plateau created by the confluence of the Rhône and the Saône Rivers: almost impossible to fractalize, it lacked the uniformly convoluted terrain that was so critical to my work in Tulle. We never went anywhere, Léon and I, except to our classes, the dining hall, the library, and the dormitory. Every day was exactly like the one before. We did well at school, but not too well. We never spoke anything but French, though I rarely spoke at all, on account of my atrocious accent. We existed in a cocoon of our own making, which turned out to be a supreme luxury, because not two kilometers away, we would later learn, at the Hotel Terminus, Hauptsturmführer Klaus Barbie was skinning and impaling prisoners (what he did if he discovered they were Jews is unprintable). Compared to the "Butcher of Lyon," Emile Vallat was a kitten.

In late May 1944, the Allies bombed Lyon before breakfast. Our school was safe, though classes were canceled for the afternoon. Nothing unusual, seeing as we were at war, nevertheless there was a change in the air. We all could feel it, a slight but significant shift in the barometric pressure of the spirit. A little over a week later, on June 6, all students and faculty were called to an assembly in the chapel. The headmaster appeared before us and proclaimed that the Lord had answered our prayers: the liberation of France had begun. Boats laden with Allied troops had already landed on the beaches of Normandy. Soon they would purge all invaders from our soil. (Were Léon and I invaders?) Already the local Gestapo unit had decamped north to provide support for their countrymen. The war was over, said the headmaster. All classes were dismissed indefinitely. We were free to go home.

One by one, two by two, parents and other relatives arrived through the many *traboules* (secret underground passages built by the silk merchants) to pick up their boys, but no one came for us. Not that we expected anyone. According to the school record, we were orphans. So we packed our few belongings, changed from our uniforms back into the plaid traveling suits Father had sewn for us, and walked off campus to discover that the war was far from over.

All pretense of collaboration finally dropped, every Resistance fighter in France now crawled out of the *maquis* and started picking off German soldiers wherever they could. The night sky filled up with fireworks, the hills reverberated with shell concussions. Under cover of all this chaos, it took us four days to walk from Lyon to Tulle. The whole time I kept thinking about the journey our parents had made at the start of the war, the distance from Paris to Tulle twice as long. We kept to the side roads and hid in the thicket during the busiest hours of the day. Panzer divisions tore up the country roads, belching diesel fumes like some Iron Age dragons. The traveling suits Father had made us provided excellent cover, as the fabric mimicked the leaf-twig-shadow pattern of the typical scrubland biome of southeastern France. Had he chosen that hideous brown-and-green plaid on purpose?

Most of the divisions were heading north in the direction of Normandy, but some, disturbingly, were heading west, in the direction of Tulle.

We scavenged food wherever we could—stolen eggs, dug-up fennel bulbs, wild cherries, edible flowers, mushrooms, and one absolutely regrettable frog (we were very hungry).

Roving bands of *maquisards* traversed the country-side, looking for fresh recruits. We hid from them as well, not wanting to be conscripted into their cause. We needed to get home as quickly as possible.

On the fourth day, not seven miles out of Tulle we spotted a farmer heading east with an oxcart loaded with whatever possessions he could gather and one tiny girl clutching a filthy doll. I remembered him from our family kitchen. He'd had an abscessed molar that was so firmly rooted in his jaw, Mother had to brace her foot against his chest to pull it out. We stepped out of the bushes and yelled for him to stop.

"Turn back," said the farmer. "There's nothing left for you in Tulle."

Five days ago there had been an uprising by the local Resistance, he explained. They had taken over the town, taken some prisoners; there were casualties among the German POWs, perhaps too many. Two days after that, a Panzer division pulled into town. In less than three hours of heavy shelling, Tulle had fallen once again. When the Germans learned what had happened to their comrades, they went door-to-door, taking every man aged sixteen to sixty (Father had just turned sixty that year!). They were rounded up in the armory, questioned, and tortured. The Germans said bullets were too good for us, shooting too honorable a death. They stopped the hangings only when they ran out of rope. Then they packed up their casualties and headed north to join their countrymen. May they all be driven into the ocean, the farmer spit into the dirt.

"What about our parents?" I said.

The farmer shook his head. "Haven't seen them in weeks."

Silently I prayed that my fractal had worked.

"You were right," Léon said to me. "We should have stayed."

"To be slaughtered like the rest?" The farmer shook his head. "Head east to Clermont-Ferrand, there's a train still running to Paris. The Red Cross will help you."

At this point Léon started sobbing, and so I was able to convince the farmer to take us at least to the train station at the outskirts of Tulle. As we crested the hill, it looked as if the streets of Tulle were filled with ants scurrying around the ruins of an anthill, hurrying to save their larvae and eggs. We climbed down and the farmer turned around and rolled away without looking back.

As we walked farther into town we could see that many of the buildings had lost a wall, exposing beds, bathtubs, kitchens, entire lives to the streets below, which were covered with rubble and giant craters. Cobblestones had been crushed under the tank treads into jagged shards. The air was hazy with the stench of burning hair. Hanging above the ruins were what appeared to be dripping tendrils of rot, as if a pernicious fungus had invaded the town, covering every light post, balcony, and tree limb. Moments later, our eyes adjusted and the tendrils resolved themselves into lengths of shredded rope. I had a savage vision of Father hanging from one of these makeshift nooses, his neck bent at a sickening angle, the skin of his face stretched tight and shiny over his purple cheeks.

Someone grabbed me by the sleeve and jerked me out of that awful reverie. It was Monsieur Hubert, our neighbor, who was sixty-eight but today looked eighty.

"What are you doing here?" I asked him. He should have been inside the fractal. Monsieur Hubert never left our neighborhood.

"I left the house a week ago," said Monsieur Hubert, "to mail a postcard to my daughter, on account of her birth."

"I didn't know you had a daughter," I said, my mind spinning with the possibility that my parents had simply *walked out* of the protective dome I had made for them.

"The house is gone," Monsieur Hubert said slowly, so as not to frighten me.

"What do you mean?" I stepped closer.

"The entire neighborhood has disappeared," Monsieur Hubert whispered. "The Germans must have developed some new kind of bomb."

"Did you find debris?" I insisted. Bombs fall short of targets all the time. My fractal wasn't strong enough; it was more an optical illusion than a pocket universe. I hadn't had the time to make more calculations, to bury my parents more deeply inside the Hausdorff dimension!

"No debris," Monsieur Hubert said vaguely. "I just couldn't find our street. . . ." He trailed off.

A man ran over and handed me a shovel.

"Come help us bury the dead," he said, "before the vultures get to them."

I handed the shovel to Monsieur Hubert, who looked at it as if I had given him a snake.

"We have to go find my parents," I said by way of apology, and pulled my grief-stung brother after me.

I led us behind the ruins of the Hotel St. Michel (yes, there was a twinge, a secret shameful desire) and took a series of shortcuts through alleys and courtyards until we got to the factory part of town. Here in the outskirts of Tulle, where it dropped off into the steep valley of the Corrèze River, all was quiet. I counted buildings arrayed around a square in the middle of which stood a statue of the Roman goddess Tutela, protector of property and persons: one, the accordion factory; two, the tire factory; three, the lace factory; four, the glass factory . . . there was the alley that led to our section of town. It was clear, no bombs; no debris.

We stepped into the entrance to the alley, and the light changed register. Up ahead, where there should have been an opening, was a dead end. But this was part of the illusion, wasn't it?

I ran to the end of the alley and put my hands on the wall. It was solid, made of the same old bricks as the factory buildings on either side. I hadn't made those bricks. But then again, I never did look down that alley on the morning we left Tulle. Had the fractal become self-propagating?

"Where's our street?" Léon wailed. "Wasn't this open before?"

A dusty rag stirred at my feet and Madame Popova's Pomeranian raised his head off his paws. He cocked his chin and blinked twice. Then he jumped to his stumpy legs and started barking. We had been friends ever since the pig snout, so this was unusual. I picked him up and immediately he stopped barking. He wriggled in my arms and I could feel that he was well fed and that his fur was clean. His eyes were bright in the dim light, and they were focused on me with an expression that said, *What took you so long?*

"Please tell me what's happening here," said Léon.

"Don't worry, he'll show us the way." I set down the dog and he started scratching at the wall. I got down on my knees beside him and put my ear to the bricks.

There was something stirring inside, like a small animal trapped behind masonry. Now all I needed to do was peel it apart, like an onion. But how to unravel a fractal? I reminded myself that fractals do not glorify complexity. They are simple structures consisting of initiator and generator, iterated over and over again.

I took a deep breath and began unraveling my spell, calculating backward, reciting all ten *sefirot* in reverse order. The Pomeranian kept digging at the wall as if he were helping (maybe he was), and soon we were able to crawl through and come out the other side.

The sky inside my artificial Tulle was a clear, cloudless blue—no smoke, no vultures. The air felt warm and damp, like the inside of a greenhouse, and smelled a little bit like compost. Not one person walked the empty streets. Cherries fallen from the trees lay rotting, undisturbed by birds, for there were none. Forgotten laundry flapped outside closed windows. The door of the bakery stood open. Some bread had been taken, but many loaves remained, most of them covered in blue-green mold. The door to the butcher shop was closed, but it was dark inside. We pressed our faces to the window and saw a whole precious chicken deliquescing into its bed of wilted parsley. Strings of sausage hung from the ceiling, writhing with maggots.

We kept walking through the deafening silence, only the sounds of our footsteps to keep us company, too afraid to speak in case we said what we both feared: something had gone wrong here. But as we reached the bottom of the staircase, we began to hear some sounds. Could it be music? As we reached the top of the hill upon which the apartment building was perched, the music grew louder. We looked up at our kitchen window and saw that it was open, with clean white muslin curtains flapping in a subtle breeze. The mellifluous strains of Chopin's Grande Polonaise unfolded into the air around us, Mother's favorite piece of music.

In Memoriam

ALIETTE TAKES AWAY THE cauliflower dish and sets down a plate of freshly baked mandelbrot.

"That's enough writing for tonight." She places her warm hand on my bald head.

"Almost finished." I remove her hand and kiss her palm, then take a bite of the cookie and notice the sharp aroma of anise among the almond and butter flavors. It's my wife's French variation, very different from how Mother used to make them. The seeds get stuck in my crowns, but I never tell her. There are many things I don't talk about with my wife. She will know everything once I'm gone. This document will reveal to her the kind of man she married.

Ninety-seven people were executed that day in Tulle. The remaining prisoners, some three hundred souls, were sent to Dachau. Only one hundred returned.

My parents survived, of course you know that. Father had faith in me and my mathematical abilities. Mother had faith in Father, so they remained close to home, as they said they would. Madame Popova stayed with them, even after her beloved Pomeranian went missing. My fractal protected them, as I had hoped it would. They were the lucky ones.

But of the dozens of people in our neighborhood who touched my life, Madame Derrasse, Vincent the butcher, and all the other people I knew by sight but not by name: I had nearly destroyed them. They left their houses, walked out of our little ghetto of a neighborhood, and were never able to find their way home again. Instead of protecting them, my fractal had extruded them, like a funnel, out of a place of safety into a massacre. That was my doing. The fact that they had survived, every single one of them, only confirms that G-d is merciful. He did not punish the neighbors for my hubris.

One person close to me did not survive that day.

By all official accounts, it was his fault. Emile Vallat had run out to welcome the Germans, to show them the Resistance snipers who were hiding on the roof of the schoolhouse, warn them of the danger, but they shot him anyway, right through the heart, the first casualty of the massacre. His mother had to wait until after all the shooting was over to drag his body out of the street. It was his doing, they said, he had it coming to him, the little collaborator. The bullet took him out as surely as a falcon plucks a dove out of the air in midflight.

Many years after Aliette and I moved to America, I took a job at the IBM research facility in Yorktown. They had developed a supercomputer that could calculate equations faster than a thousand Emile Vallats strung together with copper wire. I approached one of the technicians and asked him to run $Z=Z^2+c$ through one hundred thousand iterations, an operation that would have taken over a month had I been able to perform it without errors. By lunchtime of the following day, he brought this image to my office:

A "Mandelbulb," is what my colleagues called it. It was a joke, but the name stuck. In my heart, I called it *cauliflower*.

I asked the technician to run the same equation over one hundred million iterations, an operation that would have taken me twelve lifetimes had I performed it without breaks for sleeping, eating, breathing. The following Monday he brought me this:

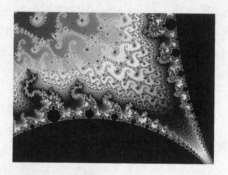

It was what I suspected all along. Everywhere you looked, the same Mandelbulb pattern repeated itself, each tiny part identical to the whole, spinning according to the proportions of the Archimedean spiral into the inner distance, into infinity, into D, the Hausdorff dimension.

Such a simple equation, $Z=Z^2+c$, with infinite iterations. One set of rules, many variations. Almost like free will itself. It's the Mandelbrot set, which is an appropriate burden for me to bear for the arrogance of my youth. Some people believe it is the thumbprint of G-d, but I prefer to think of it as a geometrical depiction of an eternally existing self-reproducing chaotic and inflationary universe.

———————

Had I been able to construct one of these universes during World War II, I could have hidden all of France. Had Emile Vallat and I been able to mend our differences and pool our calculating abilities to make a larger, more dense fractal, we could have at least saved Tulle.

Perhaps hidden inside one of those Mandelbulbs there's a version of Tulle in which Emile is allowed to grow up, mature, understand the world, set aside his hatred of others, and use his mathematical abilities for the betterment of mankind.

These days I leave the *sefirot* to the rabbis and the politics to the politicians. The math stays on the blackboard, the computer screen, the page. I no longer try to entangle monstrous mathematics with nature. That event horizon falls under the jurisdiction of G-d, who gets to decide who lives and dies. Me? I'm just an ordinary man.

About the Author

Photograph by Mette Lampcov

LIZ ZIEMSKA is a graduate of the Bennington Writing Seminars. Her work has appeared in *Tin House, Interfictions 2, Strange Horizons, Best American Science Fiction and Fantasy,* and *The Pushcart Prize XLI* and has been nominated for a Shirley Jackson Award. She lives in Los Angeles.

TOR·COM

Science fiction. Fantasy. The universe.

And related subjects.

*

More than just a publisher's website, *Tor.com*

is a venue for **original fiction, comics,** and

discussion of the entire field of SF and fantasy,

in all media and from all sources. Visit our site

today—and join the conversation yourself.